TRISTAR PICTURES PRESENTS A RICH-CREST ANIMATION PRODUCTION
A LIN OLIVER PRODUCTION A RICHARD RICH TERRY L. NOSS FILM "THE TRUMPET OF THE SWAN"
JASON ALEXANDER MARY STEENBURGEN REESE WITHERSPOON SETH GREEN
WITH CAROL BURNETT AND JOE MANTEGNA MUSIC BY MARCUS MILLER
CO-PRODUCER THOMAS J. TOBIN EXECUTIVE PRODUCER SELDON O. YOUNG PRODUCED BY LIN OLIVER
BASED ON THE BOOK BY E.B. WHITE SCREENPLAY BY JUDY ROTHMAN ROFÉ
DIRECTED BY RICHARD RICH TERRY L. NOSS

TRI
STAR
© 2000 Tiny Tot Productions, Inc. All Rights Reserved.
© 2001 Tristar Pictures, Inc. All Rights Reserved.

1 2 3 4 5 6 7 8 9 10
❖
First Edition

The Trumpet Of the Swan

LOUIE THE HERO

Text by Lin Oliver
Based on the screenplay by Judy Rothman Rofé
Illustrations by Sergio Martinez

HarperFestival®
A Division of HarperCollinsPublishers

E
OLI

Louie the trumpeter swan
wasn't like other swans.
He couldn't speak.
But Louie knew how to read and write.
He also had a real trumpet!

Louie decided to visit
his friend Sam Beaver.
He put on his slate,
his bag of chalk, and his trumpet,
and flew off to find Sam.

When Louie found his friend,
Sam was very happy to see him.

Louie told Sam all about
his new trumpet.

Sam had a good idea.

Louie could work at Sam's camp!

Every camp needs someone

who can play the trumpet.

Sam took Louie to meet

the camp director.

Chief, the camp director,
liked Louie so much
that he hired him to be
the camp bugler.

When the children at Camp Kookooskoos
met Louie, they were very excited.
They had never seen a swan
with a trumpet before.

Every morning, Louie played
a wake-up song.

Every night, Louie played "Taps,"
the tune that tells campers
it's time to go to sleep.
Louie loved his new job.

All of the campers liked Louie.
Every camper but one.

A.G. just didn't like birds—
especially birds that beat him
at volleyball.

Louie wanted to be A.G.'s friend.

But A.G. wasn't interested.

One day, when the other campers
were resting,
A.G. took a canoe out on the lake.

Paddling a canoe alone
is very dangerous.
A.G. was breaking a camp rule.
He hadn't passed his canoe test.
He hadn't passed his swimming test.

After paddling for a long time,
A.G. stopped to rest.
The waves were big.

The wind was strong.

A.G. was scared.

He knew he had made a mistake.

As he tried to paddle to shore,

the canoe tipped over.

With a splash, A.G. landed in the water.

"Help me! I'm drowning!" yelled A.G.

On the shore,
the counselors heard A.G.'s cries.

24

Sam paddled as fast as he could.

Other counselors swam.

But A.G. was so far away.

A.G. couldn't stay afloat much longer.
Soon it would be too late to save him!

But Louie had heard A.G., too.
His webbed feet moved him
across the water very quickly.

Just as A.G. sank for the last time,
Louie dove under the water.
With a splash, he came up
with A.G. on his back.

A.G. held on tight.

Louie quickly swam to shore.

That night, Chief gave a party
in honor of Louie.
Louie had saved A.G.'s life.
He was a hero!

And a hero deserves a medal.

That is exactly what Louie got.

At the end of the summer,
when all the campers left for school,
Louie flew away, too.
I had a good summer, he thought.
And how many swans have a slate,
a bag of chalk, a trumpet,
and a medal?